just add GLITTER

Angela DiTerlizzi &
Samantha Cotterill

Beach Lane Books *New York London Toronto Sydney New Delhi*

Bored, ignored, or feeling down?
Need some fancy in your town?
Want some shine upon your crown?

Just add glitter!

Try a speck,
a fleck, a sprinkle.

See how things
begin to twinkle.

A little here,
a little there.

Glitter, glitter anywhere!

Is your bedroom such a bore?
How 'bout sparkle on your door?
Could your art use something more?

Just add glitter!

A dash, a dusting,
or a touch.

It's so small but
does so much.

A little here,
a little there.

Glitter, glitter anywhere!

Are your walls asking for glitz?
Looking for more flashy bits?
Time for puttin' on the ritz?

Just add glitter!

A pinch, a cupful,
or a mound.

Glimmer, shimmer
by the pound!

A little here,
a little there.

Glitter,

glitter

everywhere!

Have you made your whole world gleam?
Do you love this glistening dream?
Then grab a ton, have fun, and scream . . .

“Add MORE glitter!”

Uh-oh. STOP.
We've got enough.
We're *lost* in all this sparkly stuff.

I thought we needed all this bling,
but it's too much of a good thing.

The glitter made it hard to see,
what sparkles most . . .

is you and me.

For Allyn, who said, "This should be a book."

—A. D.

For Aimee

—S. C.

BEACH LANE BOOKS • An imprint of Simon & Schuster Children's Publishing Division • 1230 Avenue of the Americas, New York, New York 10020 • • For information about special discounts for bulk purchases, please contact Simon & Schuster Special Sales at 1-866-506-1949 or business@simonandschuster.com. The Simon & Schuster Speakers Bureau can bring authors to your live event. For more information or to book an event, contact the Simon & Schuster Speakers Bureau at 1-866-248-3049 or visit our website at www.simonspeakers.com. Book design by Samantha Cotterill and Angela DiTerlizzi • The text for this book was set in Mrs. Eaves. • The illustrations for this book were hand drawn, paper cut, and digitally colored, then set in a 3-D environment along with the world's supply of glitter before being photographed. • Manufactured in China • 0718 SCP • First Edition • 10 9 8 7 6 5 4 3 2 1
CIP data for this book is available from the Library of Congress. ISBN 978-1-4814-0967-4
ISBN 978-1-4814-0968-1 (eBook)